NO KIMCHI FOR ME!

ARAM KIM

HOLIDAY HOUSE NEW YORK

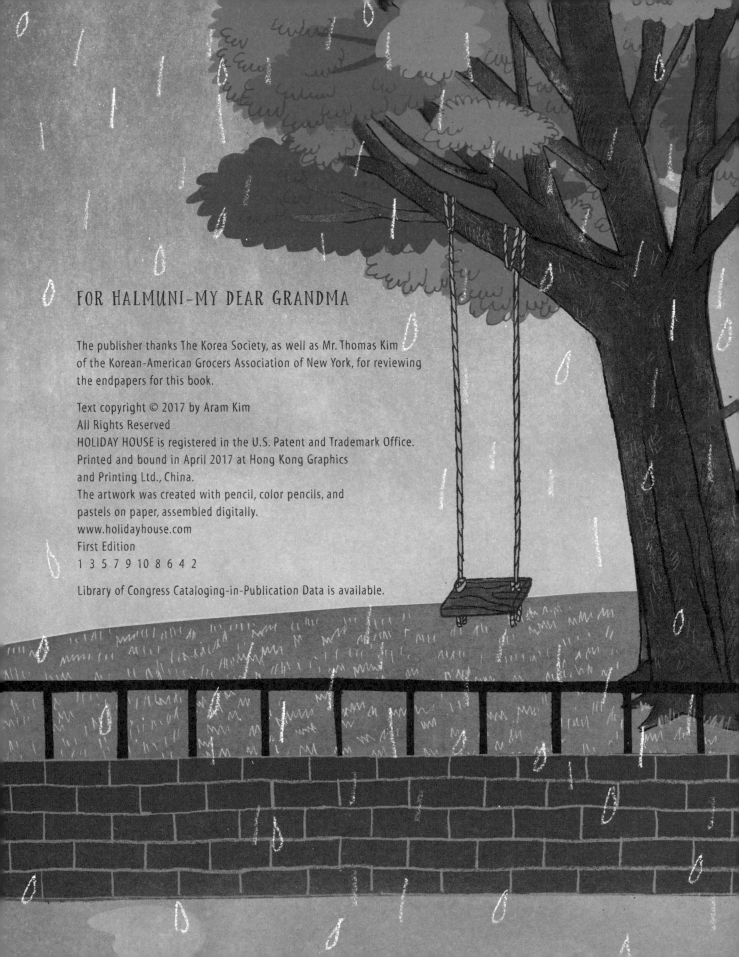

FOR HALMUNI—MY DEAR GRANDMA

The publisher thanks The Korea Society, as well as Mr. Thomas Kim
of the Korean-American Grocers Association of New York, for reviewing
the endpapers for this book.

Yoomi loves Grandma's dried
seaweed, tiny anchovies, soft
egg omelets...

even her seasoned bean sprouts!

But Yoomi does NOT like stinky spicy kimchi!

"You can't eat it because you're a baby," says Jun.

"Only big kids eat kimchi," says Yoon.

"I'll show them!"

"Oh, no."

"Yuck!"

"Baby! Baby!"
the brothers tease.

After lunch, Jun and Yoon don't let Yoomi play.

"This game is NOT for babies."

"No fair," Yoomi says.

"NOT FOR BABIES!"

"I'm NOT a baby!" says Yoomi.
"And I can prove it!"

First, she tries to hide some kimchi on a chocolate chip cookie. That doesn't work.

Then she tries to hide some on a slice of pizza. That doesn't work, either.

Ice cream doesn't work, either.

The most important thing for a clean house without mice is not to leave food on the table.

Smelling and seeing food out on the table would attract many mice and please them very

Grandma has a plan.

They chop . . .

pour . . .

break . . .

add . . .

stir . . .

Yoon smells something delicious.
"What's that?" asks Yoon.

Jun smells it, too.
"What's that?" asks Jun.

Grandma says.

Yoomi puts the fork to her mouth.

"I can do this," she says.

"**STILL SPICY**," she says.

GULP!

"But **YUMMY!**"

ABOUT KIMCHI

Kimchi is a traditional Korean dish made of fermented vegetables and seasonings. The most popular kimchi is made of Napa cabbage and seasoned with salt, red chili pepper, garlic, ginger, and other spices. Kimchi is considered one of the world's healthiest foods. It is eaten as a condiment or side dish and is also used as an ingredient in stew, soup, fried rice, and, of course, pancakes!

HOW TO MAKE KIMCHI PANCAKES

INGREDIENTS

2 cups chopped kimchi
1 cup all-purpose flour
1 cup cold water
1 teaspoon salt
1 teaspoon sugar
1 egg
(optional) 1/2 cup pork or squid, cooked and finely chopped
(optional) chopped onions

DIRECTIONS

1. Place all the ingredients in a bowl and mix well.
2. Grease a large frying pan with a generous amount of oil, and heat over medium high.
3. Spread the batter thinly in the pan and cook for 2 minutes.
4. When the bottom of the pancake gets golden brown and crispy, turn it over and cook for another 2 minutes.
5. Enjoy together with family and friends!

TIPS

1. Use sour kimchi for kimchi pancakes, not freshly made kimchi.
2. If you are using packaged Korean pancake mix, all you need is the mix, kimchi, and water!
3. Kimchi pancakes are delicious with mozzarella cheese on top! Yum.

The author thanks her mother, Eunsook Lee, for her kimchi pancake recipe.

Oisobagi

Kkaennip Kimchi

Buchu Kimchi

Baechu Kimchi

Muchae

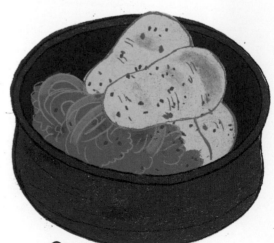

Chonggak Kimchi